JAKE

THE GARDENER

For Gabriel Ubaldini
E.S.A.

For Buddy, Ditto & Gordon Baker
D.Z.

©2006 for the English Edition Macaronic Press
© 2006 Text E.S. Aardvark
© 2006 Illustration Dirk Zimmer
Macaronic Press, P.O. Box 1542, Sebastopol, CA 95473 USA
www.macaronicpress.com

Publisher's Cataloging-In-Publication Data

Aardvark, E. S.
Jake, the gardener : guide dog digs treasure / by E. S. Aardvark ; illustrated by Dirk Zimmer. -- 1st English ed.

p. : ill. ; cm. -- (Many tongue tales)
One of a series that includes original works translated into numerous world languages.
ISBN: 0-9766859-0-6

1. Guide dogs--Juvenile fiction. 2. Urban gardening--Juvenile fiction. 3. English language--Readers.
4. Guide dogs--Fiction. 5. Urban gardening--Fiction.
I. Zimmer, Dirk. II. Title.

PS3601.A17 J35 2006
813.6
2005932848

The text of this book is set in Papyrus.
The illustrations are black line drawings with gouache watercolor.
Editor: Vivien LaMothe
Printed in Hong Kong
First English edition

JAKE THE GARDENER

GUIDE DOG
DIGS TREASURE

BY E. S. AARDVARK

ILLUSTRATED BY DIRK ZIMMER

Hi! I am Jake.
I am Granny's Guide Dog.
We take care of her granddaughter Maggie.

Maggie's Mom and Dad work day and night.

Granny says, "We will make a garden."
We go to the old gazebo.
The wind blows in from the ocean.
I smell salt and seaweed.

Granny opens the sailor's chest.
She takes out a sack full of old letters.
"Everywhere Grandfather sailed,
he sent me seeds."
I smell many strange places!

Granny smells the letters, and smiles.
Then Granny is silent.

Wind blows the letters into a puddle.

Maggie runs to save them.
The seagull cries out.
Guide Dogs do not bark at birds!

Mom says,
"Granny passed away."

I watch for her.
I wait for her.

Granny does not come home.

Mom says it is time to move to the city.
Dad brings home empty boxes.
I smell apples, and cheese, and soap.
We pack, and pack, and pack.

Dad says, "Jake is not coming.
Jake can stay with the neighbors."

But they are vegetarians!
Besides, I am a trained Guide Dog.
I am not ready to retire.

Soon the truck is all loaded up.
Mom, Dad and Maggie climb into the truck.

I slink away, my tail between my legs.
This is too much for a dog to bear.

But
what
is
this?

Maggie left the seeds!

Wait for me!

15

Dad is angry! "BAD DOG," he calls me.

"Oh, Jake! I missed you so!" cries Maggie.

"We have no room
for a dog!"
yells Dad.

Maggie says,
"Jake NEEDS
to stay here now!"

17

Mom says, "Jake will need two walks every day."
"Don't ask ME to walk him," says Dad.

Time

for

a

walk!

We

have

very

urgent

business.

19

Not many trees.
Lots of fire hydrants.
Ahh, that is better.

People, people, people.
Sidewalk, sidewalk, sidewalk.
Shops, shops, -- LOOK, a Butcher shop!

Here we go, a hole in the fence!
Smell this great dirt!

22

I like this place.
Everything we need is right here.

Granny's seeds are sprouting!
We need to plant them now.
So many holes to dig!

The grocer
gives us
water.

The butcher
gives me
meat.

Flowers open everywhere.
The smells drift through the city.

People sniff the air, and follow their noses.
In our garden they say, "This smells like home!"

27

Maggie is sick.
Mom says,
"Maggie must stay in bed."

Dad says,
"I have no time for dogs.
I need to find work!"

The morning is hot.
Our plants need water!

I pull Dad quickly
to the garden.

Two men bring a Chinese Gate, for good luck.
They ask Dad to help.

Everyone brings pieces of wood.
Dad builds a whole gazebo!

Tables are full of good food. Musicians play.
It is time for a party!

I bring Mom and Maggie to the garden.
People dance and sing. It is a wonderful party.

We come home happy and tired.
Good night, Granny.
Good night.

MANY TONGUE TALES

JAKE THE GARDENER

Follow Jake on his adventures into many languages!

FIRST EDITION BOOKS:

English, French, German, & Spanish.

Ages 3 to 8

Also good for adults

learning languages!